Detective

DAISY

The Mystery
of the
Moving
Desks

Written by Laurie Friedman

Illustrated by Barbara Szepesi Szucs

A Blossoms Beginning Readers Book

CRABTREE
Publishing Company
www.crabtreebooks.com

Level 1 Early Emergent Readers Grades PK-K
Books at this level have strong picture support with carefully controlled text and repetitive patterns. They feature a limited number of words on each page and large, easy-to-read print.

Level 2 Emergent Readers Grade 1
Books at this level have a more complex sentence structure and more lines of text per page. They depend less on repetitive patterns and pictures. Familiar topics are explored, but with greater depth.

Grade 2
veloped to tell a great story, but in a format that
by themselves. They feature familiar vocabulary

Level 4 Fluent Readers Grade 3
Books at this level have more text and use challenging vocabulary. They explore less familiar topics and continue to help refine and strengthen reading skills to get ready for chapter books.

School-to-Home Support for Caregivers and Teachers

This book helps children grow by letting them practice reading. Here are a few guiding questions to help the reader with building his or her comprehension skills. Possible answers appear here in red.

Before Reading:
- What do I think this story will be about?
  - *I think this story will be about rearranging the desks in Detective Daisy's classroom.*
  - *I think this story will be about how Daisy solves the mystery of the moving desks.*

During Reading:
- Pause and look at the words and pictures. Why did the character do that?
  - *I think Daisy eliminated Ms. Bixby from the list of suspects because she has never seen Ms. Bixby move desks.*
  - *I think Ms. Bixby was smiling because she was teasing Daisy.*

After Reading:
- Describe your favorite part of the story.
  - *My favorite part was when Daisy realized that people don't always do what you expect them to.*
  - *I liked seeing the students enjoy the surprise of the new desk arrangement.*

My name is Daisy. My friends
call me Detective Daisy.

Why? Because I'm a detective.

That means I solve mysteries.

And I'm pretty good at it.

That's what my teacher, Ms. Bixby, says.

When there's a mystery in our classroom, I'm the one who solves it.

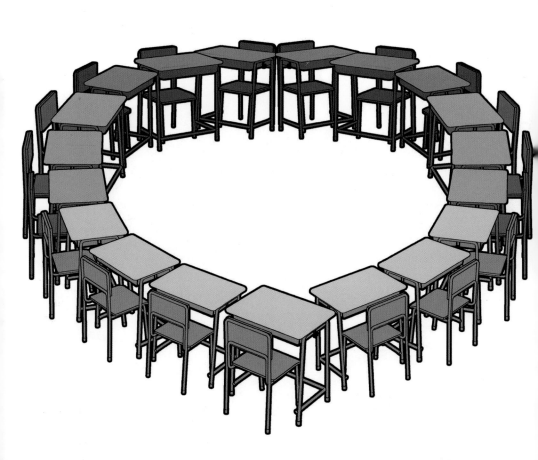

And today, there's a mystery.

The desks in Classroom 202 have been moved into the shape of a heart!

I get the heart thing. Today is Valentine's Day.

But who moved the desks? And why?

Those are questions lots of kids in my class want answered.

Like my best friend, Justin. Also Leela, Rocco, and Erin.

"Do not worry," I tell them.

I, Detective Daisy, will solve the mystery of the moving desks.

I put on my detective hat. I take out my detective notebook and pen.

Time to solve another mystery.

I start my investigation by eliminating a suspect. Ms. Bixby did not rearrange the desks.

How do I know that? Because Ms. Bixby is not a desk rearranger.

I have been learning in Classroom 202 since the start of the school year.

Not once in all those days has Ms. Bixby rearranged the desks.

Why would she start now?

Time to consider other suspects.

"Ms. Bixby, were you the last person in this classroom yesterday?"

"No," says Ms. Bixby. "But I was one of the last people."

"Ah-ha!" I say.

Whoever was in the classroom with Ms. Bixby could have rearranged the desks.

"Who else was in the classroom with you?" I ask.

"Mr. Seeger. He came in to clean while I was still here."

I think the mystery of the moving desks is about to be solved.

"Did you see Mr. Seeger rearrange the desks?" I ask Ms. Bixby.

I am fairly certain that is something she saw.

"No," says Ms. Bixby. "Mr. Seeger cleaned. Then we both left. I locked the door behind us."

"Hmmm," I say. "No one came in after you?"

"No one," says Ms. Bixby.

I scratch my chin. "How can you be sure?"

"Once I lock up, no one else comes into the classroom," says Ms. Bixby.

"Not unless there is an emergency. There was no emergency last night."

"Interesting," I say.

If no one came in after Ms. Bixby last night, then someone moved the desks this morning.

"Ms. Bixby, were you the first one in the classroom this morning?"

"Yes," said Ms. Bixby. "I was the first one in the classroom. I arrived early."

"Are you sure?"
I ask.

Ms. Bixby smiles.
"Very."

I wasn't expecting Ms. Bixby to say she was the first one in the classroom this morning.

That's because I think the desks were moved this morning.

"Ms. Bixby, did you move the desks this morning?"

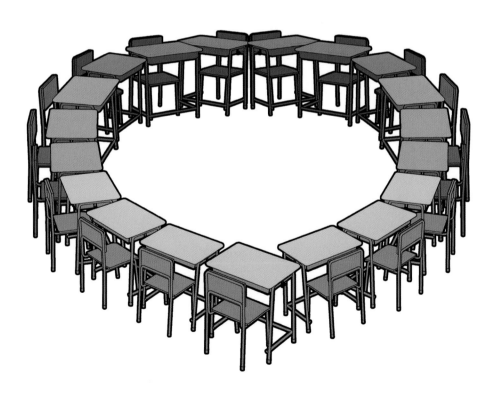

"Yes," says Ms. Bixby.

WOW!

Now I know who moved the desks. But I still do not know why.

"Ms. Bixby, why did you move the desks?"

"I read that moving desks helps students think more creatively.

I like the idea of a classroom full of creative thinkers."

Ms. Bixby smiles. "And I wanted it to be a surprise.

A Valentine's Day surprise!"

Everyone sits down at their desks.

"I like this," says Rocco.

"Me too!" says Samantha.

"Cool surprise," Justin says to Ms. Bixby.

"Yes," I say. "Very cool."

But it was not the biggest surprise.
At least not for me.

Ms. Bixby taught me an important
detective lesson.

People can change. I thought Ms.
Bixby was not a desk rearranger.

Turns out, I was wrong.

PEOPLE
CAN
CHANGE

"Thank you for the Valentine's Day surprise," I tell Ms. Bixby.

"And for the detective lesson."

"Happy to help," says Ms. Bixby.

I, Daisy, am a detective. Solving mysteries is my job.

I love doing it. And I'm pretty good at it.

But hey . . . even a good detective can always learn a few new tricks.

ABOUT THE AUTHOR

Laurie Friedman is the award-winning author of more than seventy-five critically acclaimed picture books, chapter books, and novels for young readers, including the bestselling *Mallory McDonald* series and the *Love, Ruby Valentine* series. She is a native Arkansan, and in addition to writing, loves to read, bake, do yoga, and spend time with her friends and family. For more information about Laurie and her books, please visit her website at www.lauriebfriedman.com.

ABOUT THE ILLUSTRATOR

Barbara Szpesi Szucs studied in an art secondary school, then she applied to MOME (Moholy-Nagy University of Art and Design) in Budapest, Hungary, where she got her graphic design degree. Barbara lives in a tiny village with her husband and a bunch of cute animals. They both enjoy life there, and are totally in love with nature and animals.

Written by: Laurie Friedman
Illustrations by: Barbara Szepesi Szucs

Art direction and layout by: Rhea Wallace
Series Development: James Earley
Proofreader: Janine Deschenes
Educational Consultant: Marie Lemke M.Ed.
Print and production coordinator: Katherine Berti

Library and Archives Canada Cataloguing in Publication

Available at the Library and Archives Canada

Library of Congress Cataloging-in-Publication Data

Available at the Library of Congress

Crabtree Publishing Company

www.crabtreebooks.com   1-800-387-7650

Printed in the U.S.A./CG20210915/012022

Copyright © 2022 **CRABTREE PUBLISHING COMPANY**

Published in Canada
Crabtree Publishing
616 Welland Ave.
St. Catharines, Ontario L2M 5V6

Published in the United States
Crabtree Publishing
347 Fifth Avenue, Suite 1402-145
New York, NY, 10016